Van Build _____

start date: _____

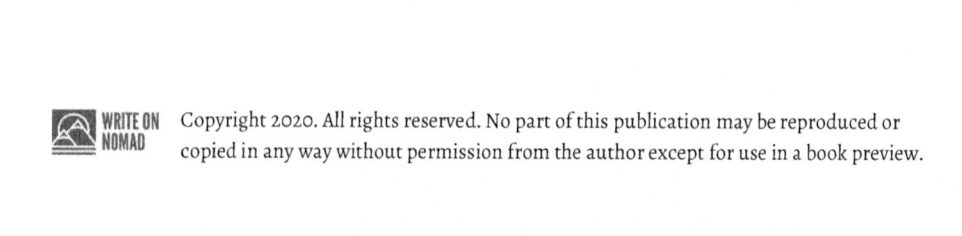

WRITE ON NOMAD Copyright 2020. All rights reserved. No part of this publication may be reproduced or copied in any way without permission from the author except for use in a book preview.

Van Build project planner workbook
every van needs a plan

Plan & Organize Your Van Build

This is your personal van build record that provides prompts, suggestions and space to chronicle your entire project. Not only a keepsake, but a practical workbook and vehicle maintenance logbook for continued reference. It also makes a handy resource for future builds and fits in a glove box. Inside, you will find five sections: Worksheets, The Van, Planning the Build, Vehicle Maintenance Log & Travel & Social:

- Worksheets to help you plan what is right for you
- Vehicle considerations
- Space to evaluate your needs & wants
- Checklists to stay organized
- Tracking sheets to know your total investment
- Vehicle maintenance logbook and more...

Save time, energy & money by following a sensible plan that you create yourself based on your unique priorities & what you value. This Project Planner Workbook will contain all your thoughts, sketches, estimates and ultimately all the details of your build in one place. Customize it and enjoy the process!

Van Build

plan
build
travel

Van Build

part I

worksheets

Designed to assist your build ♦ at the front to find easily

Van Build Shopping List
- Add items & quantities to your shopping list as you go through the workbook to keep organized with upcoming purchases
- Stay on budget by purchasing only what is needed

Time Investment Log
- Track your progress & know total hours worked

Van Build Cost Tracker
- Itemize purchases & keep a running total
- Helpful for insurance purposes
- Know your complete investment for resale

Van Build

shopping list

Add items & quantities as you plan ♦ add cost estimate if wanted

Van Build shopping list

Add items & quantities as you plan ♦ add cost estimate if wanted

Van Build shopping list

Add items & quantities as you plan ♦ add cost estimate if wanted

Van Build shopping list

Add items & quantities as you plan ♦ add cost estimate if wanted

Van Build time investment log

Date	Hours Worked	Tasks Accomplished	Total Hours

Van Build
time investment log

Date	Hours Worked	Tasks Accomplished	Total Hours

Van Build
time investment log

Date	Hours Worked	Tasks Accomplished	Total Hours

Van Build time investment log

Date	Hours Worked	Tasks Accomplished	Total Hours

Van Build

cost tracker

Date	Item Description	Item Cost	Running Total

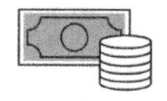

Van Build cost tracker

Date	Item Description	Item Cost	Running Total

Van Build cost tracker

Date	Item Description	Item Cost	Running Total

Van Build cost tracker

Date	Item Description	Item Cost	Running Total

Van Build cost tracker

Date	Item Description	Item Cost	Running Total

Van Build

part II
the van

An overview of the project from the beginning

This is a vehicle ♦ The shell for the build

Van Considerations

- The van as a vehicle
- The van as a shell for your build

Physical Features of the Van

- A Look at Windows, Roof & Height
- Built-ins, Weight & Emergency Exit

Lifestyle, Comfort & Vehicle Safety

- Lifestyle & Storage Considerations
- Van Type Safety, vehicle emergency checklist

Van Considerations

A vehicle & shell for the build, consider these factors:

- **Make, model & year** -do some research as some are better than others
- **Price** -budget for the vehicle & the build
- **Van price range:** $_____ Build Budget: $ _____
- **Mechanical & body condition** if the vehicle is pre-owned
- **Restoration or structural repairs** -vintage or adding height, for example
- (list any other considerations you may have)
- _____
- _____
- _____
- _____
- _____
- _____

What type of van are you thinking about choosing? This notes section is for comparisons between possible choices of vans, pros & cons list or ideas of what you seek or already have:

_____
_____
_____
_____
_____
_____
_____
_____
_____
_____
_____
_____
_____

Van Considerations

Your choice of van type makes a difference. Think about:

- Campervans have more headroom & possibly usable elements
- Cargo vans are more stealth, but you will not be able to stand up inside

Pre-Owned Vans:

- Could have extra work & time to gut the interior
- Possible disposal costs if any removals are required
- May have issues, like mold, from condensation in older campervans
- Rust-proofing or interior body repairs may present after gutting campervans or in vans previously used for work
- Consider fuel economy & van mileage if your goal is to travel extensively

How will your van be used?

What is the plan for your van? Weekends only or occasional trips? Or do you intend to live in it full time and travel? If so, do you require a rugged van, maybe a 4x4, to accommodate your adventures?

Write down your intentions or what you dream about doing with your van:

_____
_____
_____
_____
_____
_____
_____
_____
_____
_____
_____

A Look at Windows

Some vans have them, some don't. Why does this matter?

The number of windows and where they are placed in the van plays a role in determining the floorplan and layout of your space. You may want to:

- Cover them over completely, insulate & make them go away
- Have one or more installed if you don't have any at all
- Install one in the roof, as in a sunroof, especially if you choose a more stealth option for reasons of safety or privacy
- Keep existing windows, maybe tint them and use insulated curtains or insulated panels to cover them when needed

The Roof

This leads us to the roof. Is the roof flat or curved? If you intend to install a sunroof type window, you may want a flat roof. Is there anything else that you would like to have on your roof, such as a solar panel or two? Also, most vans have, or will have, a fan for ventilation installed on the roof.

A Look at Height

The height of the van inside and outside & your physical height:

- **Van interior** -by how much will the height be affected by adding insulation to the ceiling & floor and adding sub-flooring & flooring?
- **Van exterior** -will you be increasing the height with solar panels & brackets to hold them in place, roof racks, air conditioner or other?
- **Your physical height** -more important if you are tall, this may impact the design of the floorplan. You might not be able to have the bed width wise at the back, for example, so take this into account. Also, can you stand up inside?

What about built-ins?

Built-in furniture can save set-up time & help with organization:

If you purchase a pre-owned campervan, for instance, you may already have a built-in platform for the bed, or a dinette that converts into a bed. Likely there are a few shelves or cupboards as well. If you are keeping some of these elements, it may speed up the time it takes to complete your build overall. The downside is that built-ins, being permanent, determine a large part of the floorplan.

If you are designing your van from scratch, you may want to decide what built-ins would work for storage or convenience. What do you need to be able to sleep comfortably, where will you store your clothes, what about dishes? Keep in mind that when the van is moving, you will want all your belongings to be secure.

Possible built-ins may include:

- o Bed, dinette, Murphy style bed, kitchenette, closet, cupboards, shelves, under-bed storage, overhead storage, sofa

The bed can easily take up more room than anything else in the van if you go with the typical double sized bed option. Consider a few alternatives if you value your space, are a solo dweller or you are lucky enough to be able to sleep anywhere:

- o Single sized bed
- o Not having a permanent bed & using a hammock, airbed or a stretcher-style bed (canvas stretched over a frame) that can fold against a wall during the day & eliminate the need for a mattress

Weight Distribution

It is important to have the heavy items distributed evenly so as not to interfere with the handling of the van when driving. Built-ins can be heavy, as are batteries for solar set-ups, and water jugs or fresh & gray water. Consider weight when drawing your floorplan designs.

Emergency Exit

You need an emergency plan. If you have a back or side door, window or sunroof you can use for escape, keep it unobstructed & in proper working order.

Lifestyle Considerations

What type of camping do you seek?

- Campgrounds or a set location?
- Stealth camping as to not be an obvious traveler?
- Boondocking or off-road adventure?
- Short trips, lengthy trips or driving to foreign countries?

Other factors that will influence your van choice:

- How much time will you spend in the van?
- The number of people -solo, couple, couple with a baby
- Pets & how much room you can share for your pet's needs
- Will you be working as you travel -digital nomad, for example

Think about your comfort, quality of life & necessities:

- A place to sleep in comfort for many nights
- Where will you eat & do you need a place to cook
- Proper water system
- Daily personal hygiene & do you want a bathroom on board
- Workspace or leisure time area

Notes about lifestyle:

_____
_____
_____
_____
_____
_____
_____
_____
_____

Space is Limited, Essentials vs. Luxuries

List what you absolutely need & grow out from there.

What do you need to store, such as adventure equipment, and how much room will you have left after your most valued possessions are secured a spot in the van?

Van Needs	Van Wants

<u>Worksheet</u>: go to the *Shopping List* to add anything needed for the van

Van Type Safety

Basic Vehicle Emergency Items Checklist:

- ✓ First aid kit
- ✓ Fire extinguisher
- ✓ Carbon monoxide detector
- ✓ Flashlight (crank or extra batteries)
- ✓ Flares, LED flares, glowsticks
- ✓ Work gloves
- ✓ Emergency candles
- ✓ Rope, wire, bungee cords, duct tape
- ✓ Paper towels & cloths
- ✓ Maps
- ✓ Battery booster cables
- ✓ Tire pressure gauge
- ✓ Spare tire or tire repair kit
- ✓ 12-volt compressor & jack & wheel blocks
- ✓ Spare fuses
- ✓ (add other gear)
- ✓ _____
- ✓ _____
- ✓ _____
- ✓ _____

- ✓ Extra fluids such as water, motor oil, windshield washer fluid, power steering fluid, brake fluid, radiator coolant, transmission fluid, other:

_____
_____

- ✓ Basic tools like a pocketknife, utility knife (you may have to cut through a seatbelt in an emergency), screwdriver, wrench, others:

_____
_____

- ✓ Small shovel or folding shovel, snow brush, ice scraper, window squeegee, cat litter (for traction or soaking up spilled liquids)

These are suggestions & not a complete list for every situation. Go through this, fill it in and implement a safety preparedness strategy for yourself.

Van Build

part III
planning the build

An overview of the complete interior & designing

Gathering information ♦ Graph paper for planning

Checklists

- Tool checklist, Materials checklist & Building Type Safety
- Stay organized & prepared

Planning the build by sections

- Insulation, Ventilation & Air Circulation
- Power requirements & Power Consumption Worksheet
- Kitchen & Bathroom Options
- Explore ideas & make notes of what you want

Graph paper

- Refer to your notes to make scale drawings of possible floorplans
- Sketch details for better accuracy, put your ideas on paper
- Extra pages can be used for pictures or van vision board

List of Best Reference Materials

- A go-to list of favorite websites & books to remember

Van Build

tool list

Checklist of all the tools needed for the build

Measuring Tools	Hand Tools	Power Tools
Tape measure	Hacksaw	Jigsaw
Level	Pliers	Circular saw
Carpenter's square	Miter box	Drill
Plumb bob	Hammer	Router
Chalk line	Screwdrivers	Nail gun
	Stapler & staples	Sander
	Clamps	
	Wire cutters	
	Files	
	Caulking gun	

Suggestions to get you started, fill in essential tools for your build.

Worksheet: go to the *Shopping List* to add needed tools

Van Build

materials list
Checklist of all the materials needed for the build

_____	_____
_____	_____
_____	_____
_____	_____
_____	_____
_____	_____
_____	_____
_____	_____
_____	_____
_____	_____
_____	_____
_____	_____
_____	_____
_____	_____
_____	_____
_____	_____
_____	_____

Suggestions to get you started, materials will depend on your unique build. Be as specific as you can when listing your materials:

Adhesives, nails, screws, hardware, wood, sandpaper, steel wool, caulk, paint, sawhorses, wiring, electrical supplies, lighting, insulation, plumbing supplies, whisk & dustpan... This list will help you gain a clear idea of what you are building and estimate materials needed to do the job.

<u>Worksheet</u>: go to the *Shopping List* to add needed materials

Building Type Safety

Basic Safety Equipment Checklist:

- ✓ Dust mask
- ✓ Safety glasses/goggles
- ✓ Safety shoes/boots
- ✓ _____
- ✓ _____

- ✓ Ear protection
- ✓ Work gloves
- ✓ Disposable gloves
- ✓ _____
- ✓ _____

Note: This is in addition to the Basic Vehicle Emergency Items Checklist earlier in the book, so you will already have a first aid kit and other essentials if you assembled this list of gear.

Other safety recommendations:

Read labels & follow instructions for all products. Things like adhesives and paint can be toxic and a van is a small space.

- ✓ Consider more environmentally responsible options when available
- ✓ Handle correctly wearing proper protection, like mask & gloves
- ✓ Use products as directed by the manufacturer and ensure you have adequate ventilation
- ✓ Dispose of unused portions responsibly or share with a buddy

Always have a professional Electrician install wiring or check your wiring job and solar set up. This is a serious aspect of a build and can be a fire hazard if not installed properly.

Even if you are new to building, you can learn to do it yourself with the multiple resources available in books or online. If this is out of your range, seek assistance and don't take unnecessary risks.

Keep in mind that a quality build can allow for long-term comfort in a safe and healthy environment.

Planning the Build

What is the motivation for my van build?

Knowing your focus for the project will help you to make good decisions regarding the build more quickly and easily. There are many choices for building materials and having a clear goal will allow you to zero in on appropriate choices. Your focus may be:

Health

Personal health issues, stress or environmental allergies may be good reasons for a van build to gain more control over your environment or personal circumstances. If health is your focus, you might consider natural over synthetic materials or environmentally friendly alternatives. Deciding to eliminate toxic materials will simplify your product choices.

Best Choices

If you are looking to make your van build the best possible for as long as possible, you will want to choose durable options that make the most sense to you overall. This eliminates low quality, quick-fixes and places your focus on quality.

Quickest

Your circumstances may require your van build to be done as soon as possible. In this case, your choices could be based on materials that are easy to find and install. This style of build can also be a work in progress, where you get enough done now to get you out on the road with plans to add more amenities over time. Using this Project Planner Workbook as you go will help you hold on to ideas and drawings until you are ready to continue with your build in the future.

Most Economical

For some, the least expensive method will be the focus. This may be the case if you have an older van with a limited lifespan or a first build to try out the lifestyle. A budget-friendly build might rely on recycled, salvaged or thrift store finds. Also, look at clearance sections or scratch & dent items at stores. Be cautious of damaged materials, mold or mildew.

Come back to your focus if you get stuck to guide your choices.

Insulation, Ventilation & Air Circulation

Important for personal comfort & health and the longevity of your van

Your van is a vehicle and not a building. When it comes to this topic, remember that your outside walls are made of metal. Be aware of why this makes a difference as you go through your research of materials and the best approach for air quality and temperature control.

Moisture & Condensation

Humidity inside the van comes from your body, cooking, heating, wet laundry, pets and the atmosphere. If it stays trapped, you will eventually have issues with corrosion of the van from the inside, mold and mildew.

Start with keeping everything as dry as possible. Also, what types of things store moisture? Look at bedding and your mattress. For example, cotton absorbs moisture and foam doesn't. You can't prevent moisture, but you can prevent it from becoming a problem. Write down the areas where moisture could collect in the van that you can check regularly for dryness or damage.

_____
_____
_____
_____
_____

Insulation

The purpose of insulation in a van is to keep the temperature more comfortable, and to reduce road noise and vibration when driving. There are numerous points of view on this subject regarding materials and techniques. This section will allow you to work through some of the challenges and find solutions that work well for you. Because of differences in climate and individual comfort, there isn't a straight answer that works for all situations. Fill in these worksheets to better decide on materials and a strategy.

Do I need a vapor barrier?

Opinions differ here but remember that you are essentially building inside of a metal box that does not allow moisture to escape. Because of this, you may view the van itself as a vapor barrier. This is all about moisture control and preventing corrosion issues, mold and mildew. Do you have a method that can seal up your wall completely if you go with a vapor barrier? This is a key decision. After doing some research, record your thoughts or ideas regarding how you would like to approach this part of the build.

_____
_____
_____
_____
_____
_____

Where to insulate

If you are going for full insulation in the whole van, you may use different types of insulating materials depending where it is going. All insulation is going to take up some of your interior space, so look closely when planning how this is impacting the size. This is a list of the most common places to insulate and why. Record your thoughts on how you want to insulate these areas:

Floor -this can help greatly with road noise, vibration and some for temperature, especially in colder climates -usually a thinner material is better to preserve valuable height

_____
_____
_____
_____
_____

Ceiling -mostly for temperature reasons -hot air rises, so insulation can guard against some heat loss through the roof -the sun hits the roof first & can really heat up the inside, so it can work to protect you -thicker insulation here can be beneficial if you have the height

_____
_____
_____
_____
_____

Walls and Door Panels -mainly for temperature -most of your insulation will be here -the most critical areas, insulation must be installed correctly, or it won't work effectively & may cause problems later -be aware of thickness

_____
_____
_____
_____
_____

Windows -temperature -using insulated panels or curtains will help a lot to protect against the heat of the sun or heat loss through the windows -reflective insulating materials are useful and can be incorporated into your panel or curtain designs to be reversible for maximum benefit -don't forget about a sunshade for the windshield

_____
_____
_____
_____
_____

Insulating Materials

When shopping for insulation, remember that air quality is an issue in a small space. Some factors when choosing insulating materials:

- Availability of products
- Time -how long will it take to get materials & how long to install?
- Ease of use -do you have curves in the walls or roof to work with?
- Cost -total of the types used
- Does the product flex or will it deteriorate with movement?
- Product toxicity -look at natural materials when possible
- Thickness & use -do you require an air space with it or not?
- Do your chosen materials absorb moisture or wick it away?

Notes about insulation & materials:

_____
_____
_____
_____
_____
_____
_____
_____
_____
_____
_____
_____
_____
_____

Popular choices include wool batting, cork, various types of rigid foam board, spray foam for gaps and reflective materials.

Tip: if using rigid materials, make cardboard templates first for accuracy of cuts & save them for finished walls and floors later in the build (label them!)

Ventilation & Circulation

Proper air flow will go a long way toward keeping your space dry and comfortable. When it becomes stale, or you are operating a gas heater, the air needs to be vented outside. Considerations for ventilation & circulation:

- Roof fan -very popular option, particularly in hot weather or when cooking -some available with a cover for use in the rain -may be viewed as essential for ventilation
- Vent holes -creating vent holes in your built-ins and ensuring that you have good air flow under the bed and throughout the van prevents moisture from getting trapped anywhere & causing problems
- Fan -in addition to a roof fan, something like a 12-volt box fan helps a great deal with circulating warm air that otherwise stays up high near the ceiling and helps with dryness in those nooks & crannies
- Magnetic screens -making or purchasing screens for your windows or side door may be useful for airing out the van

Heat Source

In colder climates, you will have to have a source of heat. There are many 12-volt heaters on the market that use propane, butane or kerosene gases. You must always have a window open to vent fumes when using gas! Other options to stay warm are 12-volt electric blankets, electric heaters and woodstoves.

Ideas about ventilation, air circulation & heat:

_____
_____
_____
_____
_____
_____
_____

Power Options

Wiring and Electrical

Take an inventory of everything you will need electricity to power. Include all the electronics you require for business, communication and entertainment. Here are a few suggestions to get started, add what is missing for you:

- Laptop computer(s)
- Cell phone charger
- _____
- _____
- _____
- _____

- Fan or air conditioner
- Interior lights
- _____
- _____
- _____
- _____

Energy conservation is a crucial first step when traveling or being off grid. For this reason, finding alternatives to electricity when possible is welcome. For example, solar desk lamps can be charged outside during the day to use in the evening. Alternatively, using low consumption options such as LED lights are a leading choice. They are bright, safe and energy efficient.

Power Choices

There are four options in a van: solar, shore power, generator & a second battery charged by the alternator. Knowing what you are going to go with will allow you to have any wiring installed now before continuing with the build. This part will require research and possibly some assistance if you have never worked with electricity.

Power Consumption

No matter what you choose, getting familiar with how much power you consume will be necessary for you to calculate in order to design a system to meet your demand. The Power Consumption Worksheet on the next page has plenty of space for you to compare products, or for new calculations if you change appliances.

Power Consumption Worksheet

If your power is coming from batteries, either from a solar set-up or a second battery that is charged from your alternator, you will need to know your total power consumption measured in amps. Batteries are measured in amp hours and a battery should never be drained more than fifty percent. The calculation for this is: Watts ÷ Volts = Amps. You may also need: Volts x Amps = Watts.

To calculate your power consumption in watt hours (Wh), you take the wattage of the appliance and multiply by the daily hours of use.

Appliance or electronics	Wattage of appliance	(x) Daily hours of use	(=) watt hours (Wh)
(example) light bulb	100 watts	10 hours/day	1000 Wh

You will need your power consumption total in order to calculate the size of the battery bank you will require. Once you get into your research for batteries, this will make more sense. This is meant to be a place for you to calculate and record this data, so you have it on hand for later.

Notes about my electrical requirements

Write down information from your research that you want to use:

Kitchen & Bathroom

What do you need for daily living?

Main considerations

The kitchen and bathroom go together as they have shared water considerations. The main elements to look at here are a fridge, stove, sink, toilet and shower. Also, your water system and storage for both fresh and gray.

Fridge & stove -some people choose to forego both in favor of using a cooler and cooking outside with a camp stove or over a fire -your lifestyle and location will affect your choices, so think about:

- o Do you want a cooler or a fridge?
- o Will you be cooking at all inside of the van?
- o How much food do you need and how long do you need to store it cold?
- o What method of power are you using for your fridge or stove or both?

What options are you leaning toward?

_____
_____
_____
_____
_____
_____

Sink, toilet & shower -these may be luxuries or necessities depending on your situation -water and disposal are the major decisions here:

- o If you cook, you will have dishes to wash
- o Daily grooming -brushing teeth & keeping yourself clean
- o Keeping your living space clean & your pet
- o Do you want a toilet on board? What type of toilet could work for you & how will you dispose of the waste?
- o What about a shower set-up? Is this important for you to have?

Looking at the sink, toilet & shower, what do you feel is essential? Write your ideas & thoughts:

_____
_____
_____
_____
_____
_____

Water -this is a big consideration as it is essential to life -make sure you have enough -points about water:

- Have an idea as to how much water you use in a day to be prepared
- Water filtration is essential for most, bacteria can be deadly
- Consider your water when placing heavy items around the van for even weight distribution
- Are your water containers easy to take out & refill?
- Is your gray water easily accessible to remove & dispose?

Write your ideas here for water needs, storage & disposal:

_____
_____
_____
_____
_____
_____
_____
_____
_____
_____
_____
_____
_____
_____

Floor, Walls & Ceiling

Floor

This can be as straight forward as a two-part process or a more complex four-part process, depending on your climate & length of time you will be spending in the van.

- o Noise reduction -optional but a sound deadening treatment will help to quiet road noise
- o Insulation -not required for all but helpful in colder climates
- o Subfloor -needed for support of your finished floor
- o Floor -your finished flooring, the nice-looking part!

A common subfloor is a sheet of plywood. Ideas differ, but a thinner sheet is adequate in a van. Less thickness is desirable here and you don't have to be concerned about supporting heavy furniture like you would in a house. Finished flooring materials include laminate, painted wood, bamboo, vinyl or cork. Choose what makes you happy. This is getting into the fun part of customizing your space. How do you see your floor?

_____
_____
_____
_____
_____
_____
_____
_____
_____
_____
_____
_____

Walls & Ceiling

Often, thin plywood is used to cover the insulation on the walls and ceiling. It is flexible and allows for some shaping when working with curves in the van. This can be painted or sealed with natural oils or some other creative treatment. Making cardboard templates first can assure more accurate cuts. Label your templates for better organization. You could use a fancier wood if you like. How do you see the finished walls and ceiling? Any ideas for colors or overall themes?

_____
_____
_____
_____
_____
_____
_____
_____
_____
_____
_____
_____
_____
_____
_____
_____
_____
_____
_____
_____
_____
_____
_____
_____
_____

The personal touches

Interior design

This is the creative part that may have inspired you to start a van build in the first place. The necessities are thought out, what about the details?

- Shelves or fabric storage pockets
- Cupboards and drawers
- Clothing storage or closet
- A place for shoes & boots
- Special focal point of interest or decorations

Often, these are the customized details that become a focal point in the van. Having even a couple of nice pieces in a small space will add a lot of personality. What do you really want in your van?

_____
_____
_____
_____
_____
_____
_____
_____
_____
_____
_____
_____
_____
_____
_____
_____
_____
_____
_____

Collecting your thoughts

A summary of your information before the floorplans begin

- Van considerations -modifications, restorations or repairs
- Window placement, roof shape, height
- Built-ins -adding or subtracting any
- Weight distribution of heavy items
- Emergency exit
- Planning in space for emergency gear -easy & accessible
- Interior space used for insulation & wall thickness
- Height used for insulation & ceiling and floor
- Placement of larger items if using -fridge, stove, sink, toilet
- Daily living -bed, sofa, shelves, cupboards

Sketching your ideas

Referring to your lists above will assist you in making sketches by keeping in mind where you have windows, for example, and to plan by drawing those in first.

There are sheets of graph paper on the following pages. It is a light gray color, quarter inch square (1 square = 0.25" or ¼"). Use it for possible floorplans, ideas or detail drawings. It is best to do scale drawings for floorplans for accurate finished results. There are really only a few ways to arrange a van interior, but even a classic layout can be an outstanding build with the right amount of creativity.

Having all your information together in this workbook including your sketches will provide you with a wealth of ideas and reference materials when the time comes to start building your van. There are also pages to list your favorite websites, books or outside sources for how-to information and guides. You can fill this in and have this list available to you now for the original build or later if you want to make changes to your van in the future.

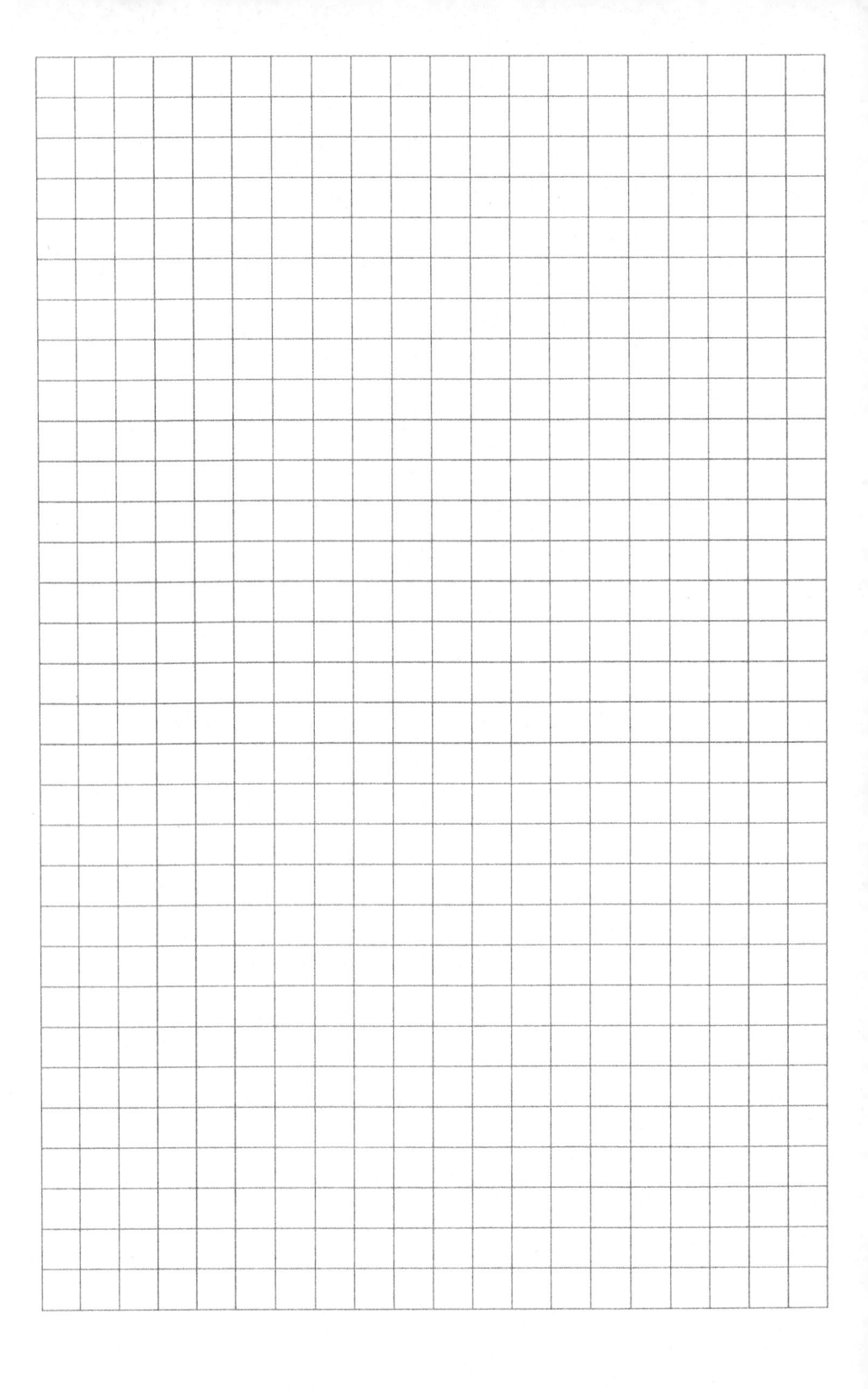

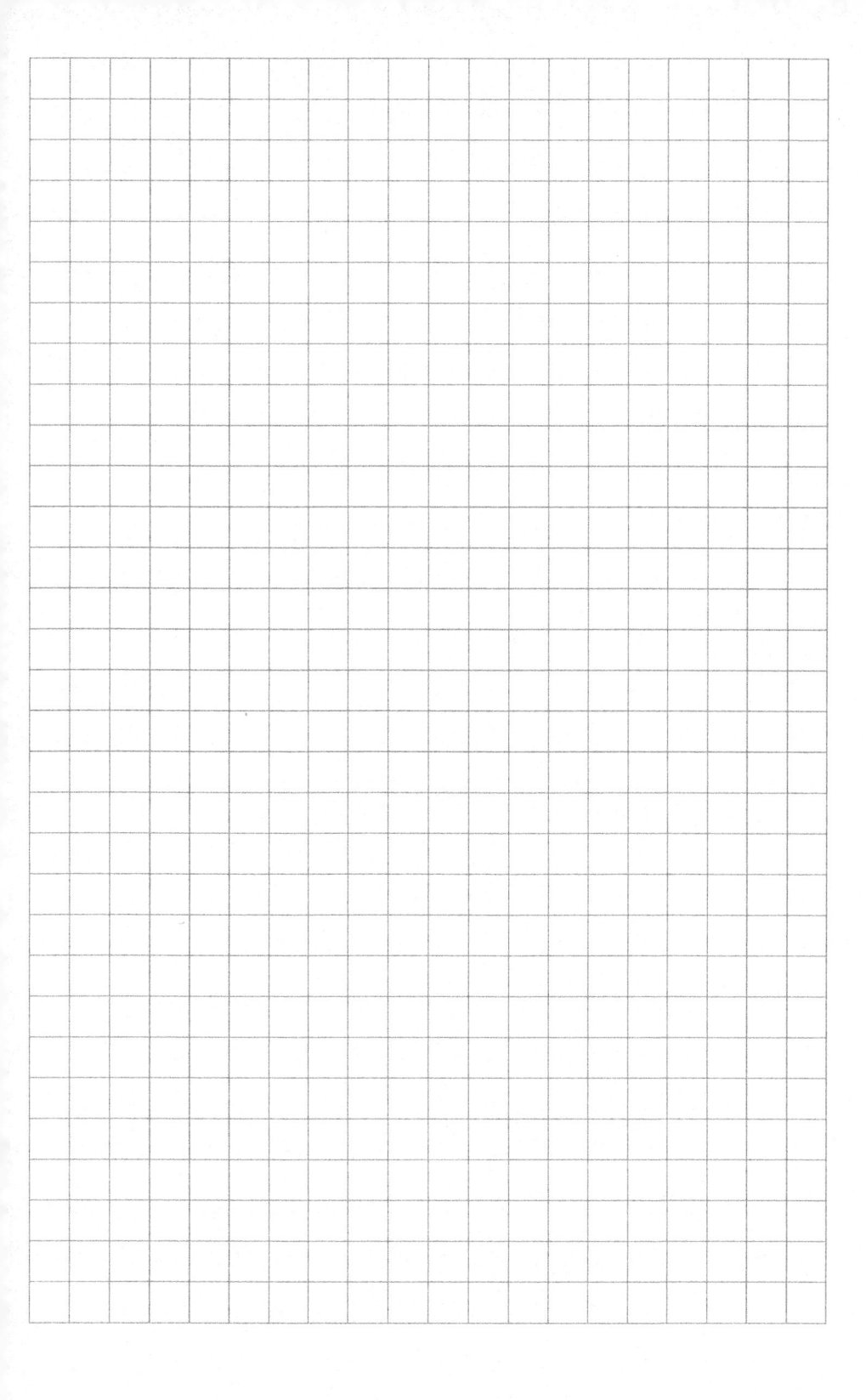

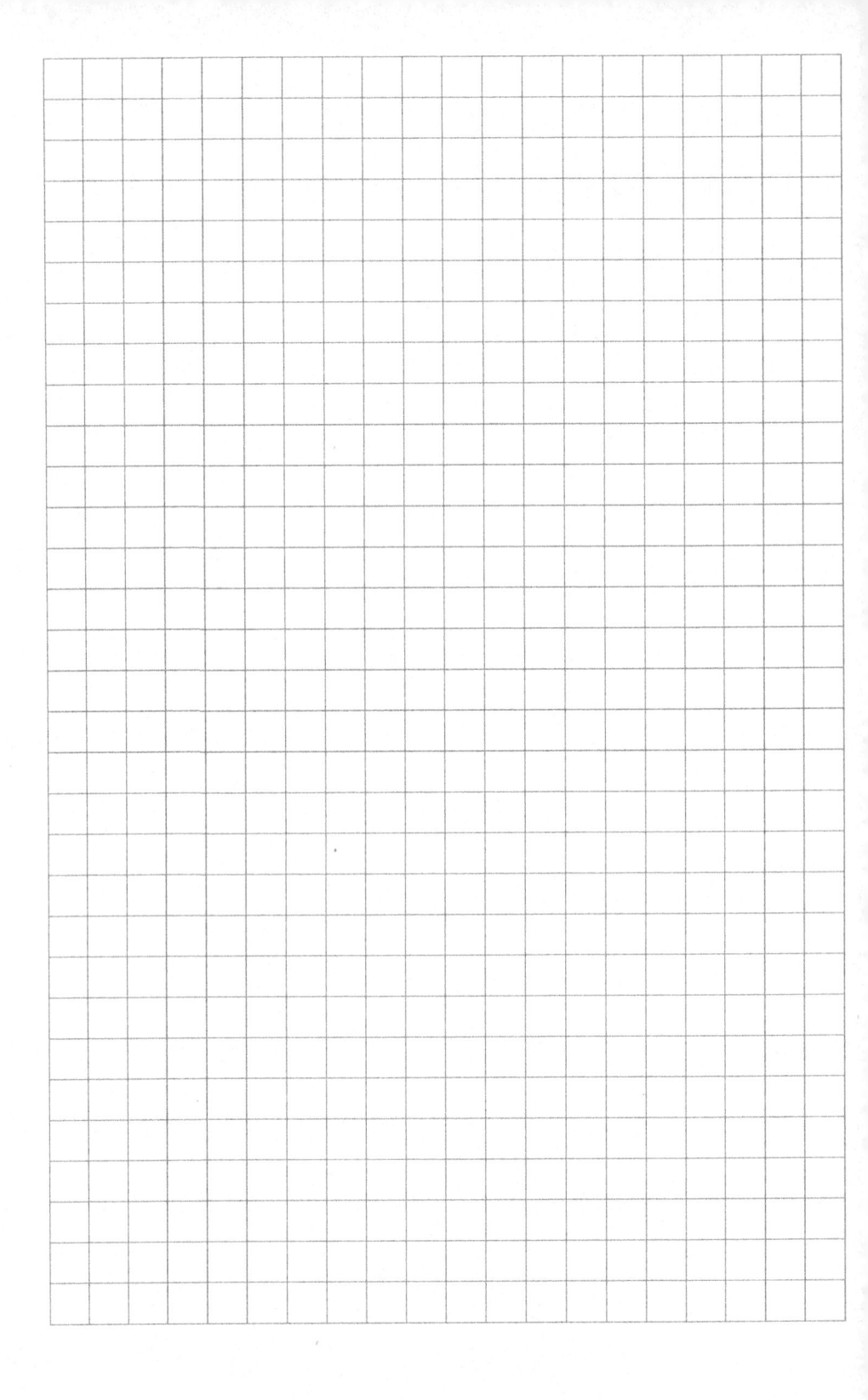

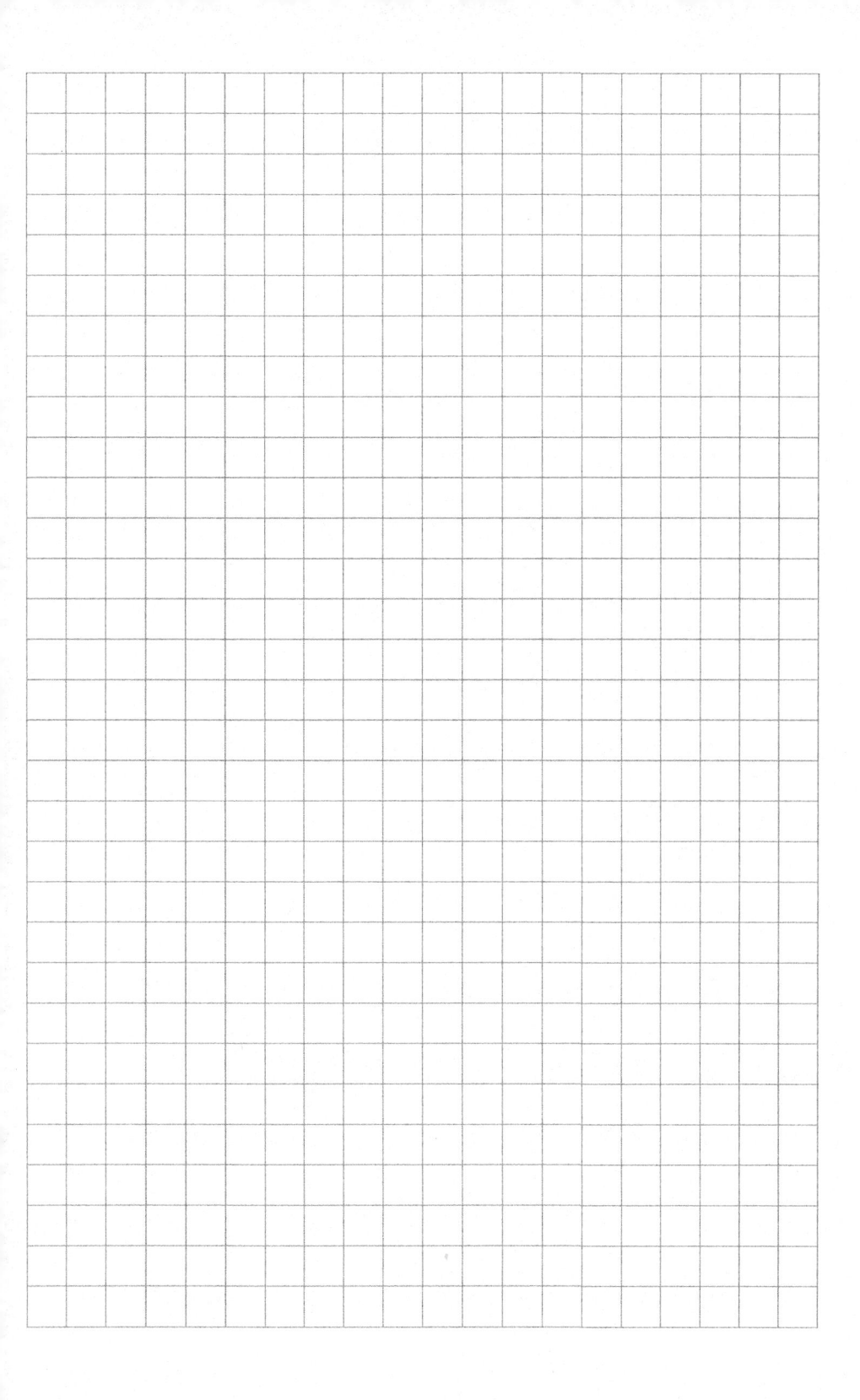

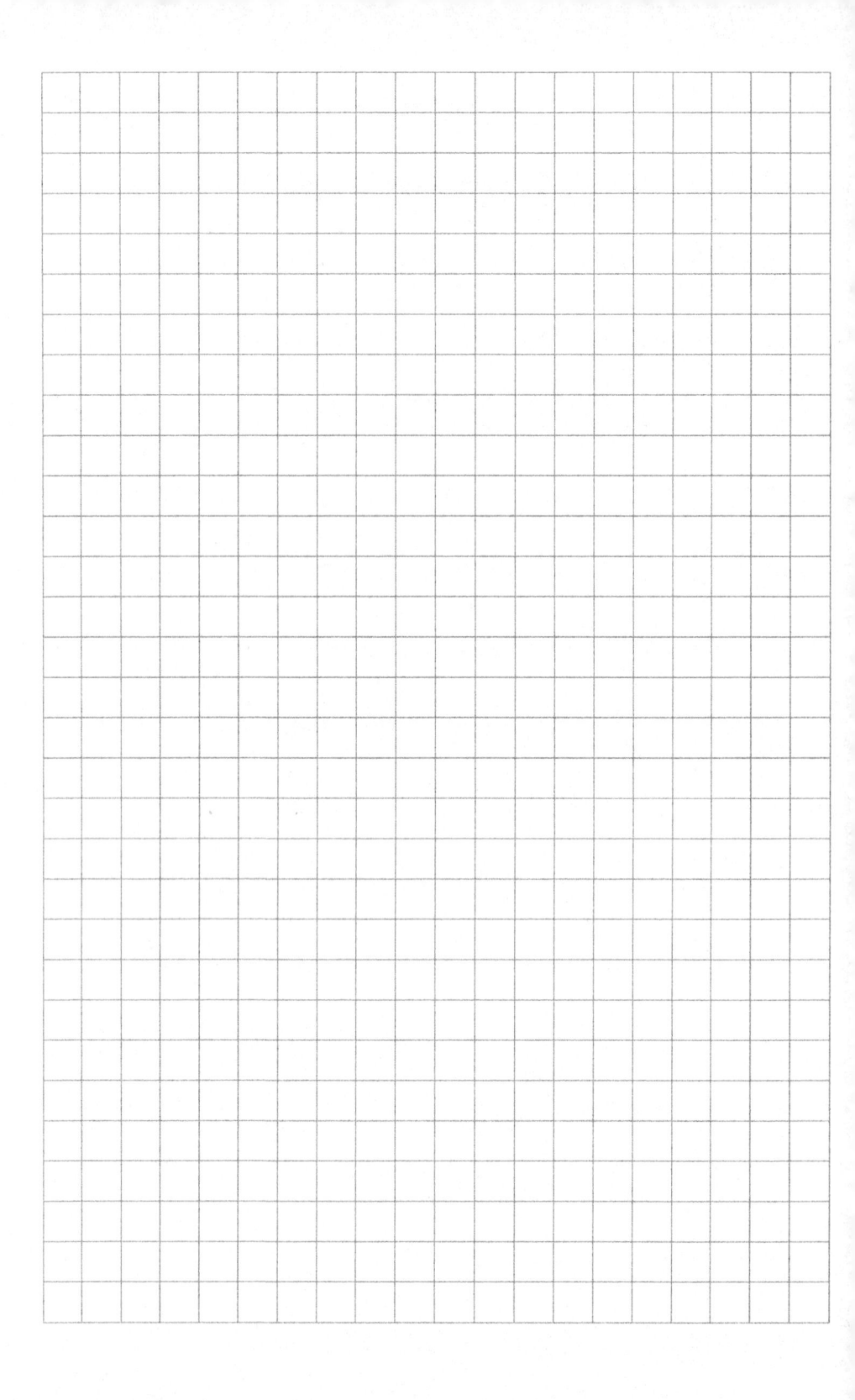

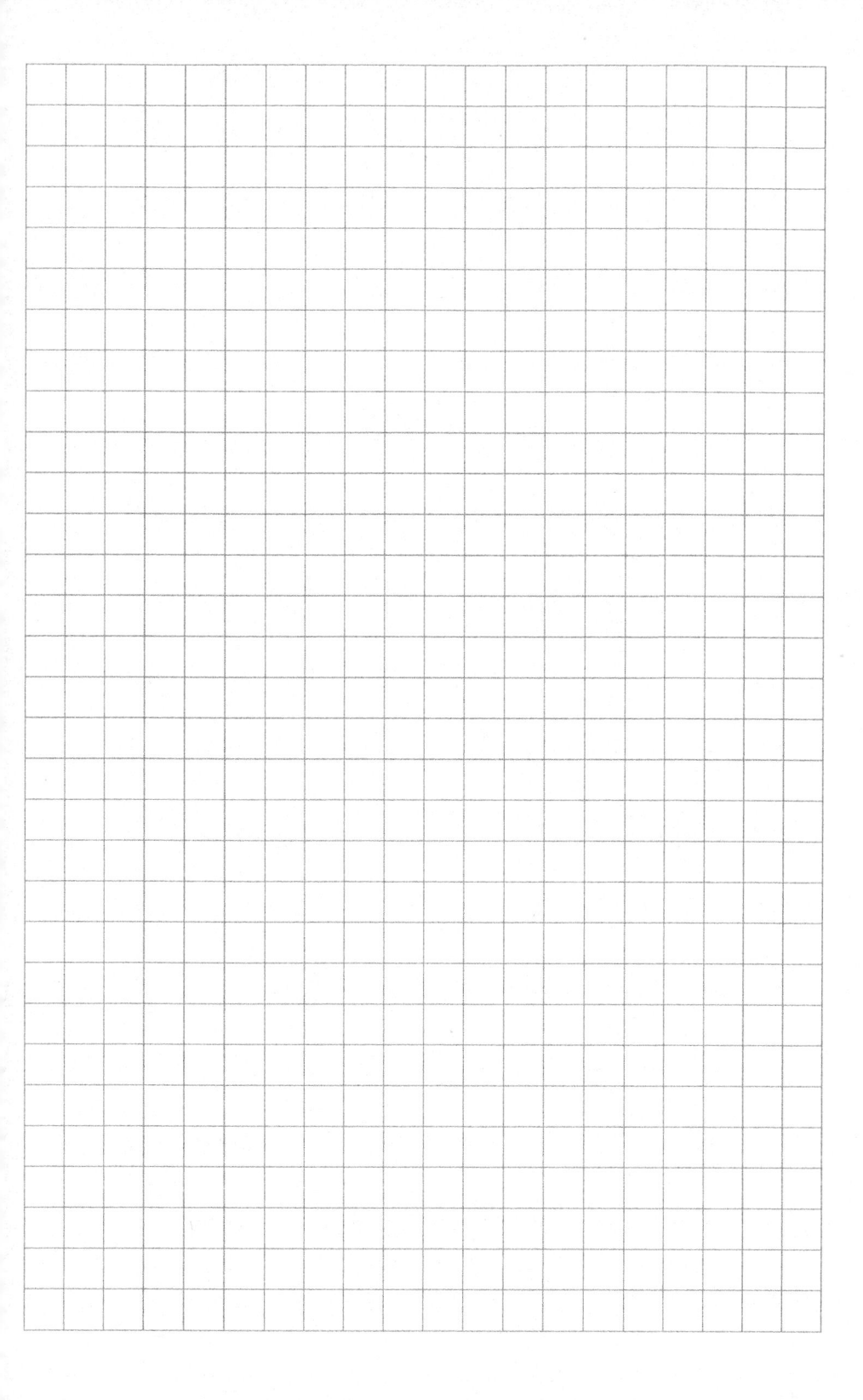

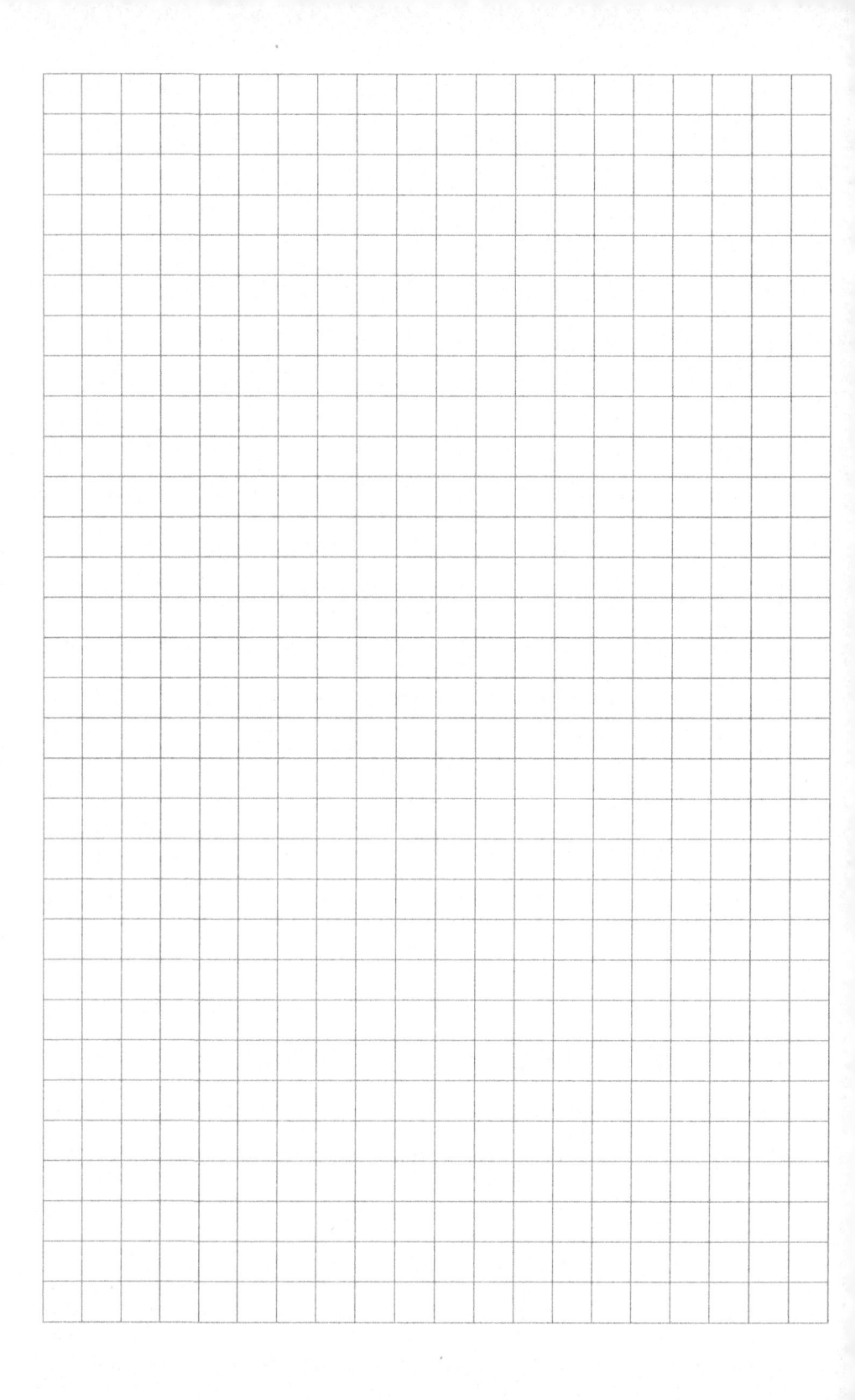

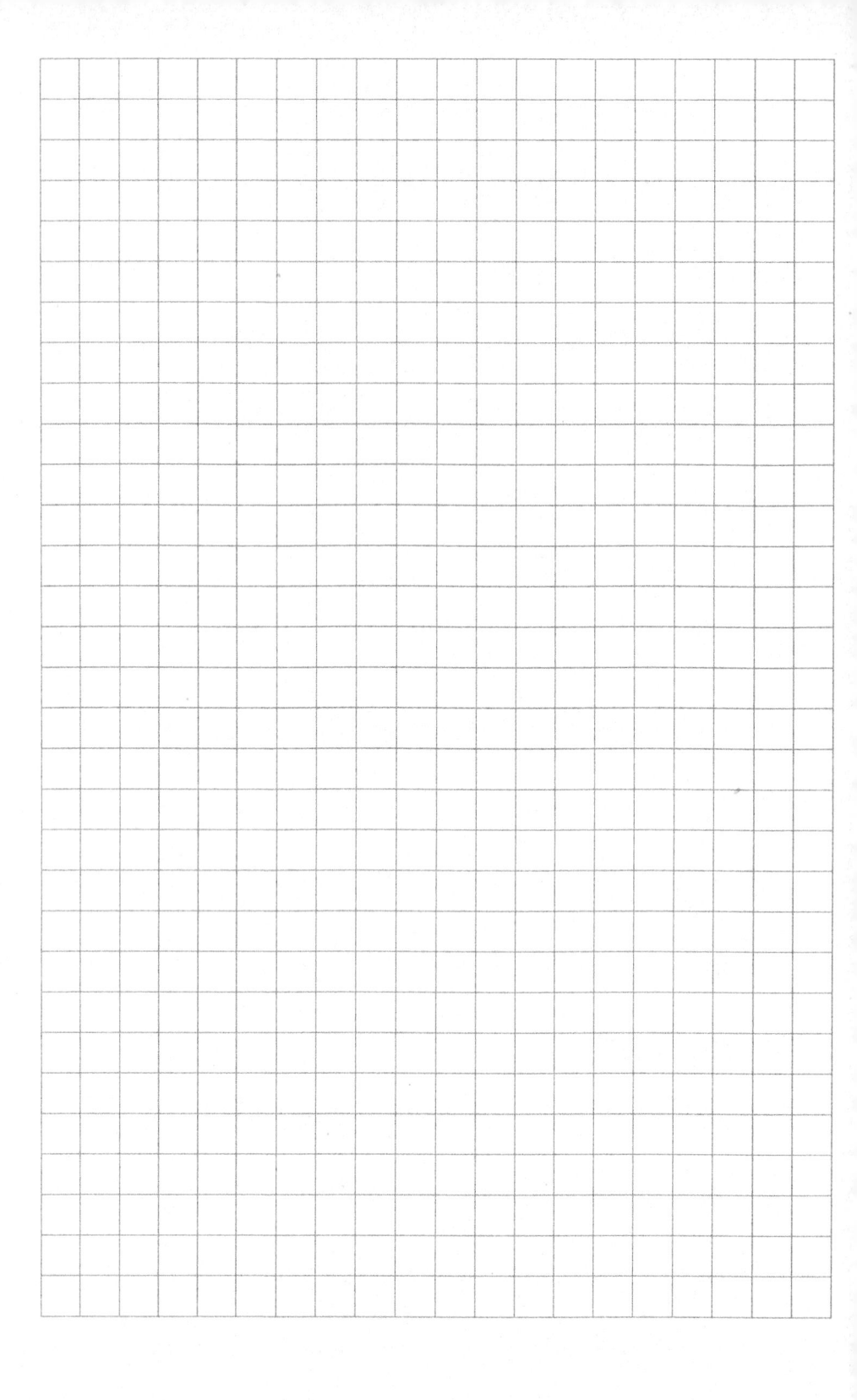

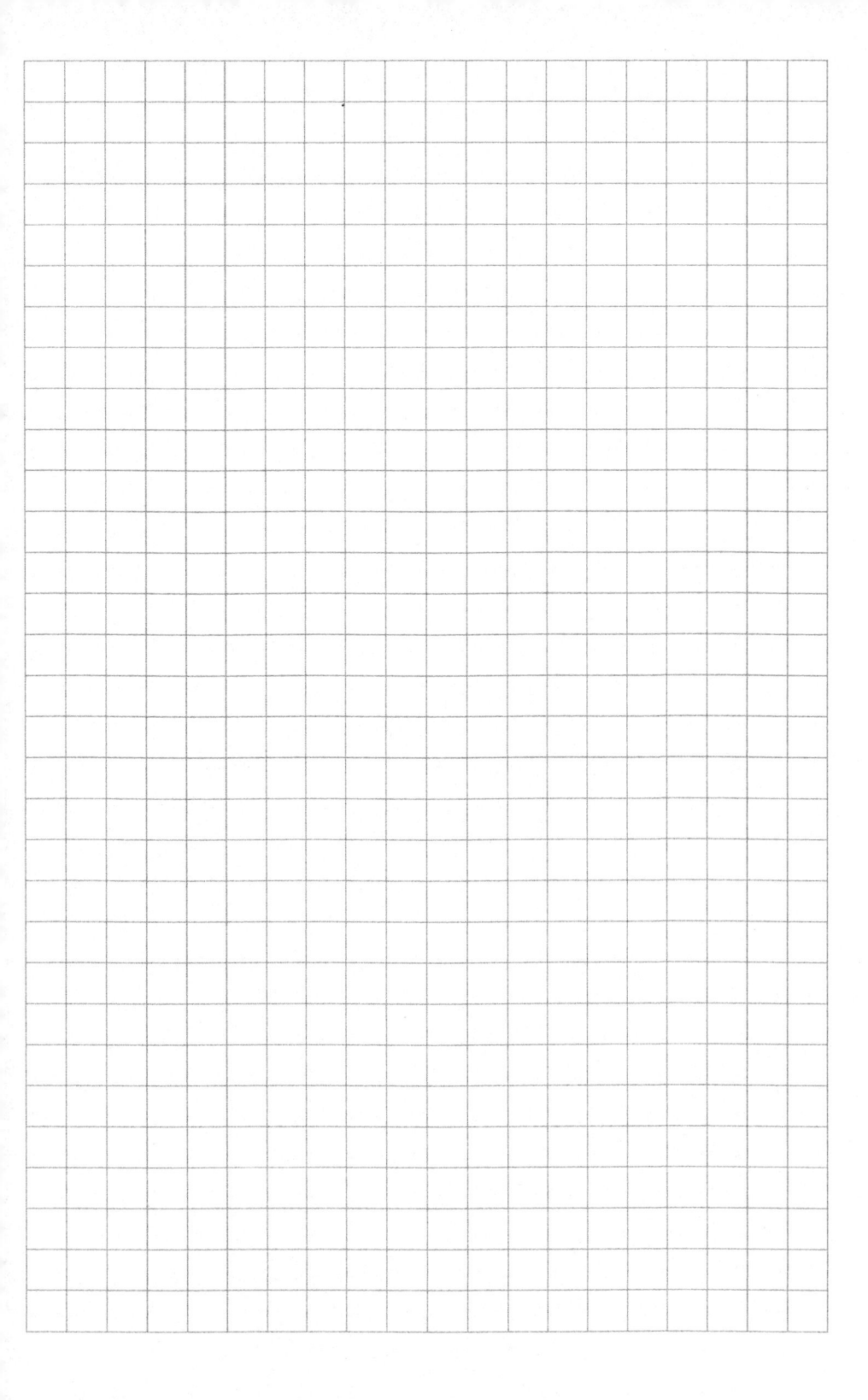

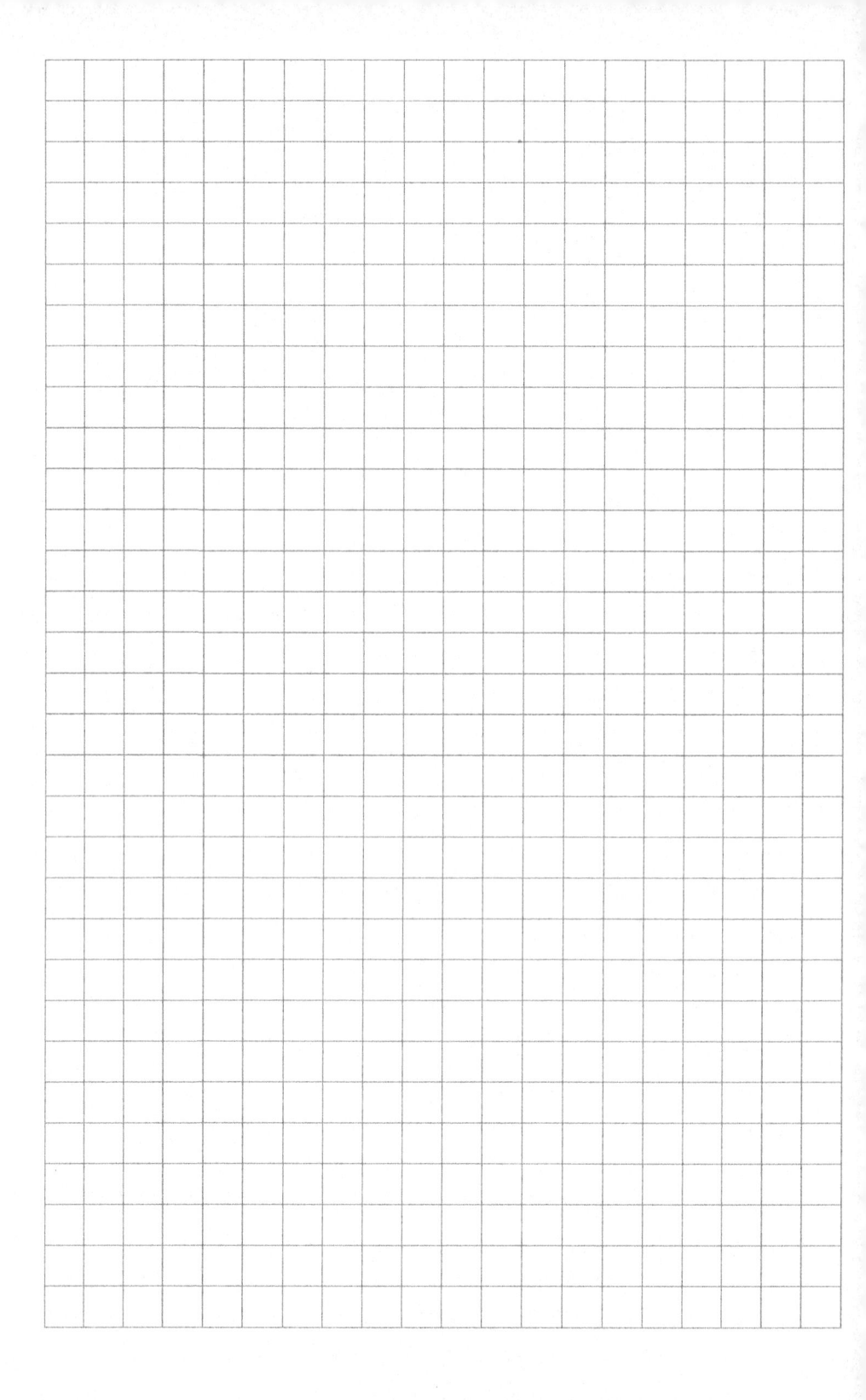

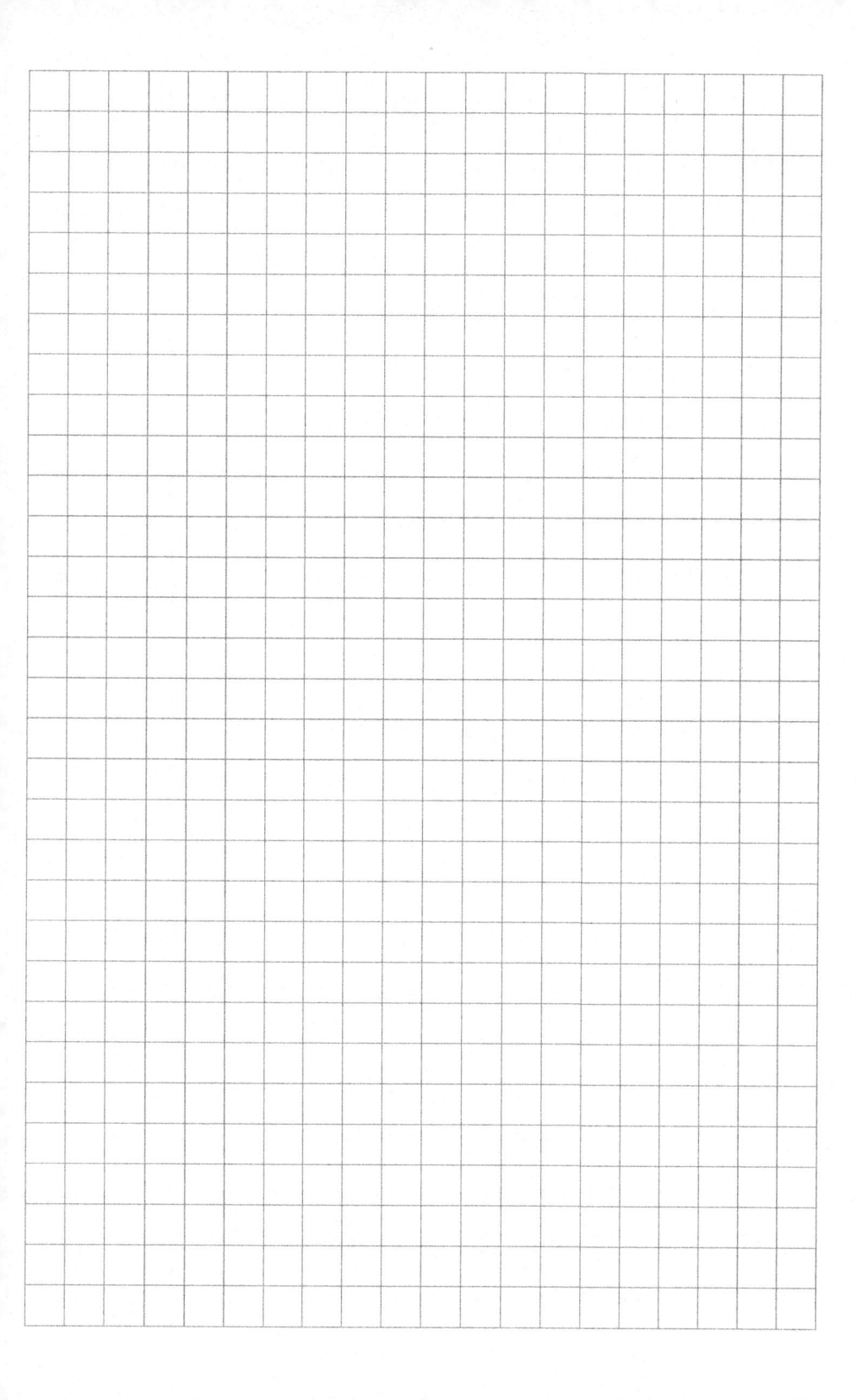

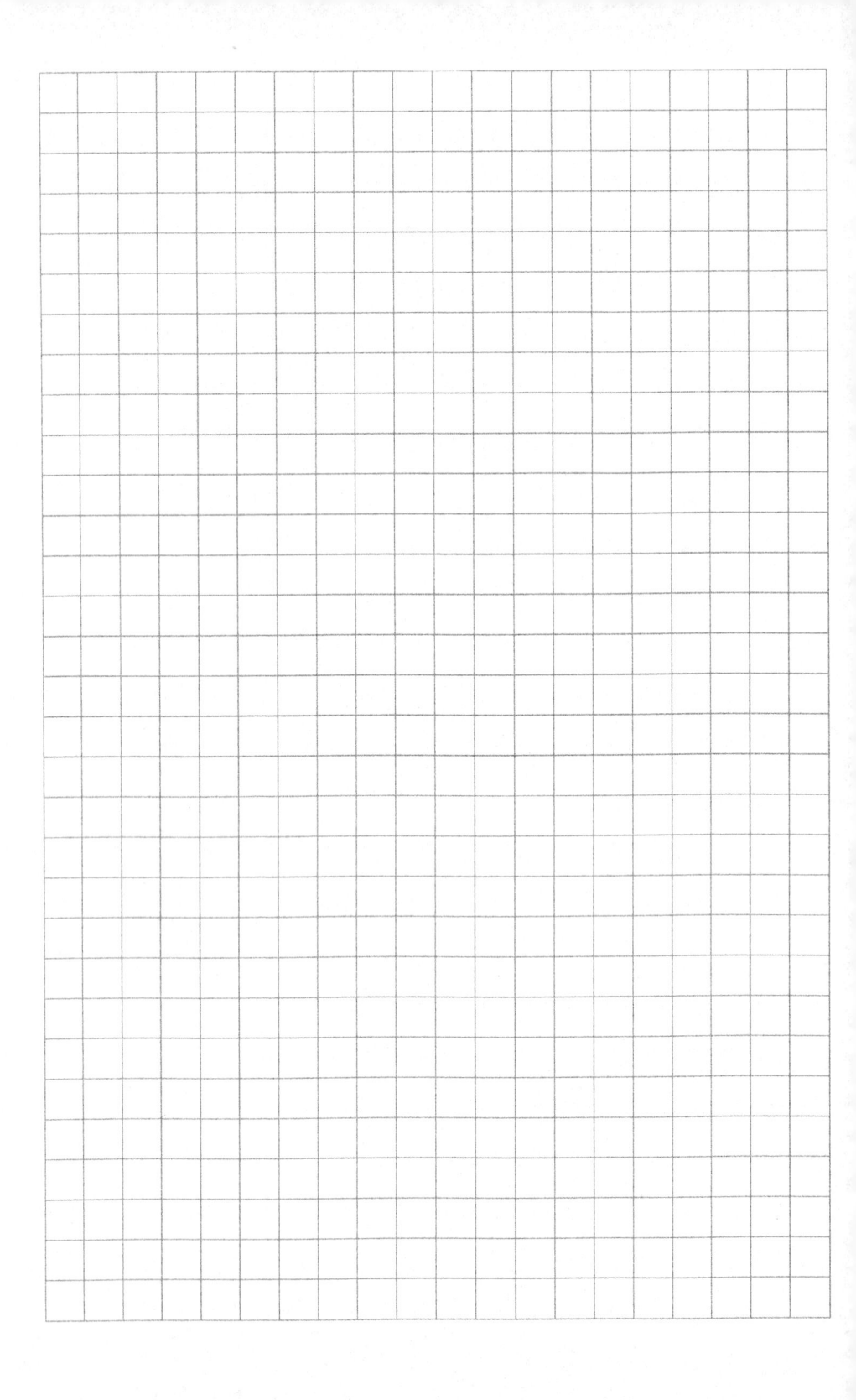

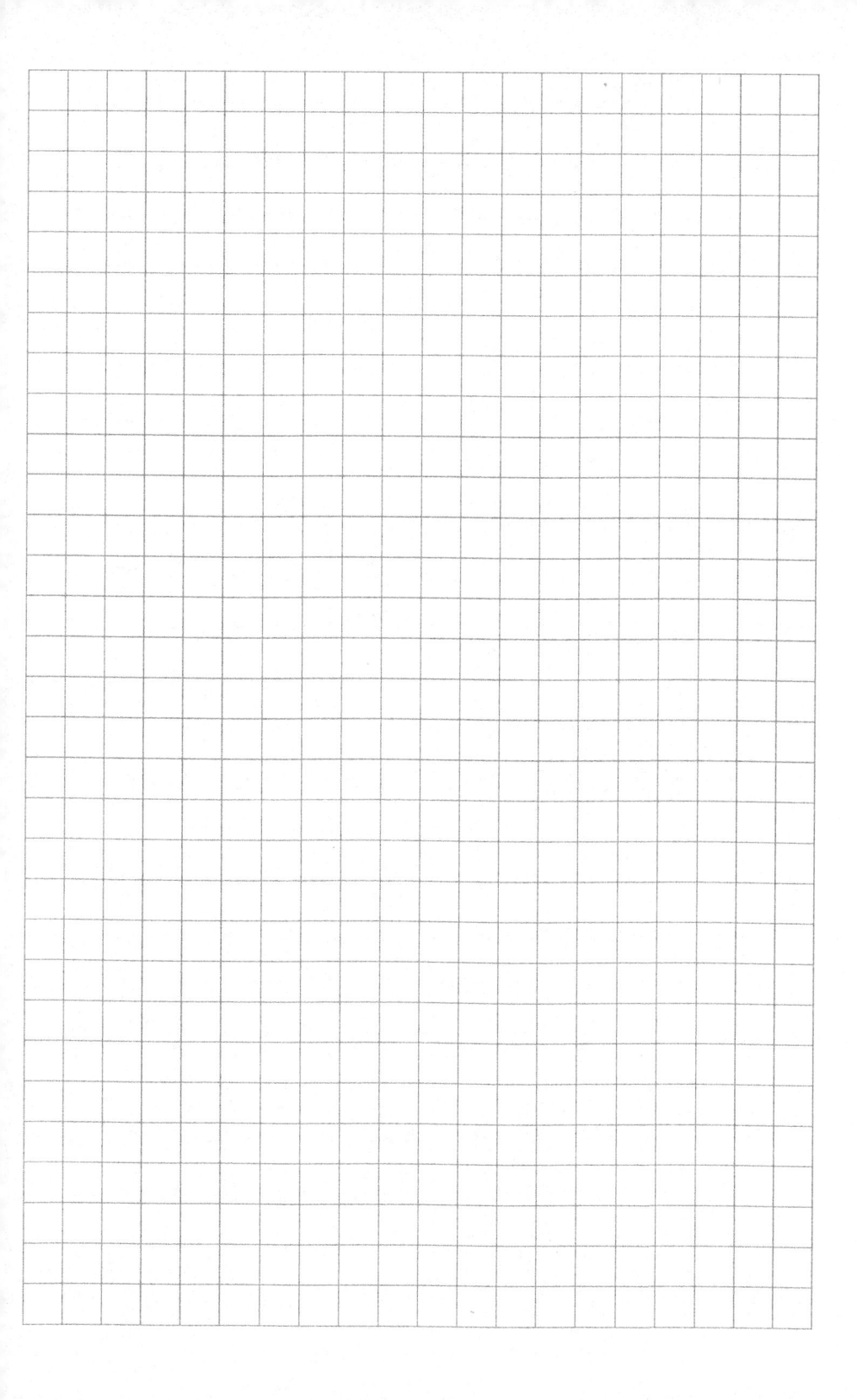

Best Websites, Books & Reference Materials

Favorite building guides, instructions & inspirations

Website, Book or Reference	Type of Information

Best Websites, Books & Reference Materials

Favorite building guides, instructions & inspirations

Website, Book or Reference	Type of Information

Mechanics & Vehicle Technicians

Name	Contact information

Van Build

part IV
vehicle maintenance log

Maintain & Prevent ♦ Vehicle & Travel Safety

Contact List

- List of trusted mechanics & technicians for repairs & service

Monthly Checklist

- Suggested list of things to inspect regularly for wear & tear and working condition

Maintenance Log

- Create a complete record of all services performed on the van including oil changes, tire rotations & regular tune-ups
- Know the dates and costs of repairs for possible warranties

Travel Safety & Contacts

- Make a list of family or friends to have handy in an emergency
- Consider your personal safety on the road

monthly checklist

Check or Inspect	J	F	M	A	M	J	J	A	S	O	N	D
Headlights												
Brake lights/taillights												
Hazard lights												
Windshield wipers												
Tire pressure & inspection												
Air filter												
Battery inspection												
Hoses & belts												
Emergency exit												
Motor oil												
Windshield washer fluid												
Radiator coolant												
Power steering fluid												
Transmission fluid												
Brake fluid												

Check mark if you have no concerns, make a note if it needs attention:

_____
_____
_____
_____
_____

monthly checklist

Check or Inspect	J	F	M	A	M	J	J	A	S	O	N	D
Headlights												
Brake lights/taillights												
Hazard lights												
Windshield wipers												
Tire pressure & inspection												
Air filter												
Battery inspection												
Hoses & belts												
Emergency exit												
Motor oil												
Windshield washer fluid												
Radiator coolant												
Power steering fluid												
Transmission fluid												
Brake fluid												

Check mark if you have no concerns, make a note if it needs attention:

_____
_____
_____
_____
_____

maintenance log

Date	Description of Service	Shop	Cost

maintenance log

Date	Description of Service	Shop	Cost

maintenance log

Date	Description of Service	Shop	Cost

maintenance log

Date	Description of Service	Shop	Cost

maintenance log

Date	Description of Service	Shop	Cost

maintenance log

Date	Description of Service	Shop	Cost

maintenance log

Date	Description of Service	Shop	Cost

maintenance log

Date	Description of Service	Shop	Cost

maintenance log

Date	Description of Service	Shop	Cost

maintenance log

Date	Description of Service	Shop	Cost

Basic Travel Safety Checklist

For on the road, boondocking & out of country travel

- ✓ Hiding spot -in the van
- ✓ Hiding spot -remote location
- ✓ Pet health documents
- ✓ _____

- ✓ Travel insurance
- ✓ Photocopies of important documents
- ✓ Regular check-in buddy
- ✓ _____

Contacts (family & friends)

Name	Contact Information

Just the simple act of staying in contact with someone on a regular basis can go a long way toward your safety & security. Having a hard copy of your contact list can be useful if your cell phone is not available.

Van Build

part V
travel & social

Great Places ♦ New Friends

Places to Remember

- Make your personal list of best places to camp, dine, surf or bike, these are places you want to see again

Travel Notes

- A brief section to record events & stories of people & happenings along your journey

Van Mini Guest Book

- A fun way to remember the people you entertain & new friends that you meet

Places to Remember

Along your travels you are bound to stumble across hidden gems you will want to keep in mind for future. Make notes about where they are and why they are great. Maybe for the scenery, internet connection, best camping or amenities.

Location	Reason to Remember

Places to Remember

Location	Reason to Remember

Travel Notes & Stories

This is a section for you to hold memories of things that happen along the way, places you have seen and people or characters you have encountered.

Van Mini Guest Book

welcome

leave your name & comment

Name	Comment

Van Mini Guest Book

welcome

leave your name & comment

Name	Comment

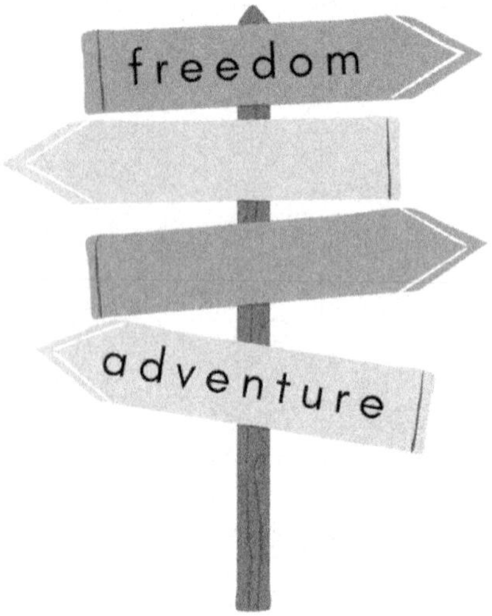
freedom
adventure

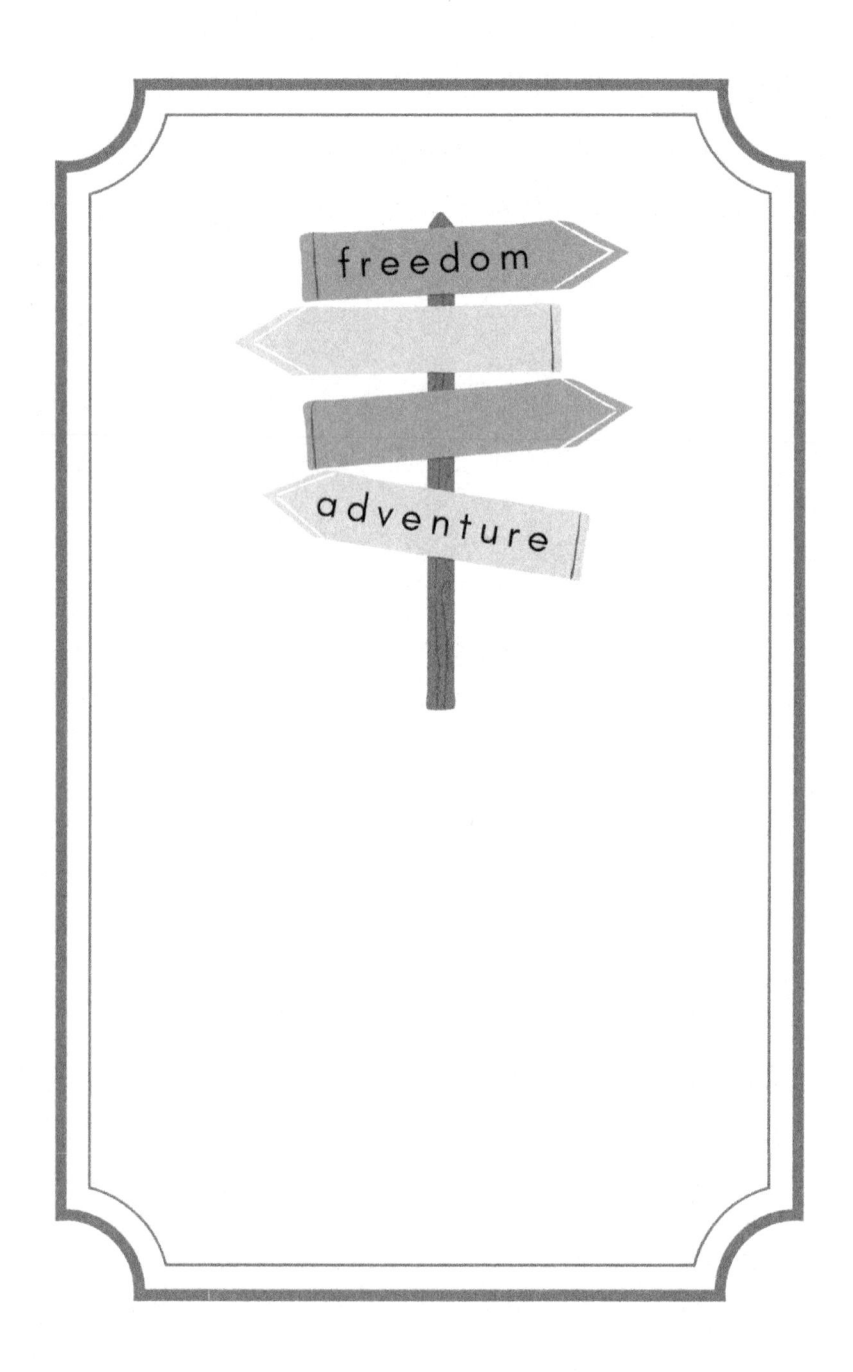

Printed in Great Britain
by Amazon